DOWNHILL RACERS

JONNY ZUCKER AND IAIN BUCHANAN

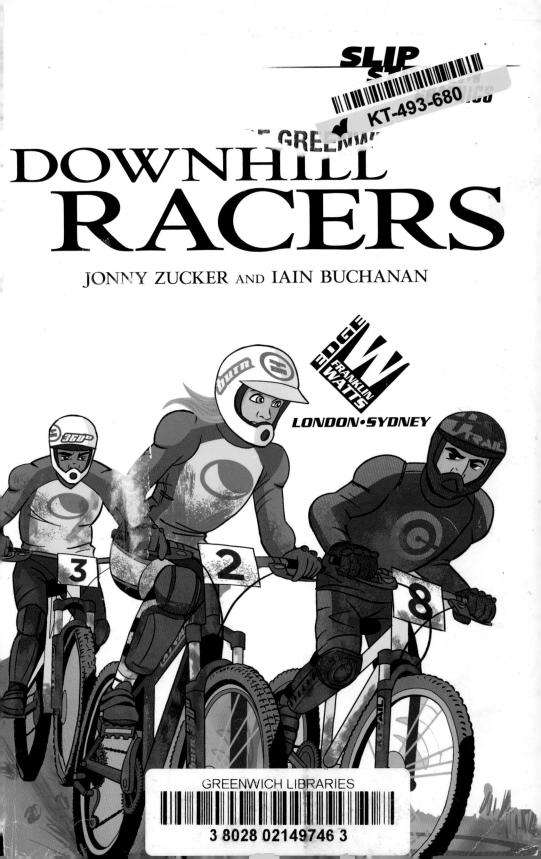

EDGE
FRANKLIN
WATTS

LONDON•SYDNEY

DOWNHILL RACERS

Sam and Liz cycle for Glasgow Giants.
Sam is club captain.

The Giants' biggest rivals are Sterling Wolves.
Their captain is Rocky Moore.

The downhill league final race is on Sunday
morning at Fort William. All racers arrive at Fort
William Youth Hostel on Friday afternoon...

First published in 2014 by
Franklin Watts
338 Euston Road
London NW1 3BH

Franklin Watts Australia
Level 17/207 Kent Street
Sydney, NSW 2000

Text © Jonny Zucker 2014
Illustrations © Franklin Watts 2014

The rights of Jonny Zucker to be
identified as the author and Iain Buchanan
as the illustrator of this Work have
been asserted in accordance with the
Copyright, Designs and Patents Act, 1988.

A CIP catalogue record for this book
is available from the British Library.

ISBN (pb): 978 1 4451 3089 7
ISBN (Library ebook): 978 1 4451 3094 1

Series Editors: Adrian Cole and Jackie Hamley
Series Advisors: Diana Bentley and Dee Reid
Series Designer: Peter Scoulding

A paperback original

1 3 5 7 9 10 8 6 4 2

Printed in China

Franklin Watts is a division of
Hachette Children's Books,
an Hachette UK company
www.hachette.co.uk

FOR TEACHERS

About

SLIP STREAM

Slipstream is a series of expertly levelled books designed for pupils who are struggling with reading. Its unique three-strand approach through fiction, graphic fiction and non-fiction gives pupils a rich reading experience that will accelerate their progress and close the reading gap.

At the heart of every Slipstream graphic fiction book is a great story. Easily accessible words and phrases ensure that pupils both decode and comprehend, and the high interest stories really engage older struggling readers.

Whether you're using Slipstream Level 2 for Guided Reading or as an independent read, here are some suggestions:

1. Make each reading session successful. Talk about the text or pictures before the pupil starts reading. Introduce any unfamiliar vocabulary.

2. Encourage the pupil to talk about the book using a range of open questions. For example, what would have happened if Sam hadn't swapped his bike with Rocky's? What else could Sam have done?

3. Discuss the differences between reading fiction, graphic fiction and non-fiction. Which do they prefer?

For guidance, SLIPSTREAM Level 2 – Downhill Racers has been approximately measured to:

National Curriculum Level: 2b
Reading Age: 7.6–8.0
Book Band: Purple

ATOS: 2.1*
Guided Reading Level: I
Lexile® Measure (confirmed): 360L

*Please check actual Accelerated Reader™ book level and quiz availability at www.arbookfind.co.uk